SpongeBob SquarePants

SPONGEBOB'S SLAP SHOT

by David Lewman
illustrated by Harry Moore

SCHOLASTIC INC.
New York Toronto London Auckland Sydney
Mexico City New Delhi Hong Kong Buenos Aires

Stephen Hillenburg

Based on the TV series *SpongeBob SquarePants*® created by Stephen Hillenburg as seen on Nickelodeon®

ISBN-13: 978-0-545-12703-5
ISBN-10: 0-545-12703-3

12 11 10 9 8 7 6 5 4 3 2 1   9 10 11 12 13 14/0

Printed in the U.S.A.

First Scholastic printing, March 2009

"He shoots! He scores!" shouted SpongeBob as he swept a napkin into a trash can. "And the crowd goes wild!"

He flicked another piece of garbage into the can. "Watch this, Squidward!" he called. "I never miss! Not a blob of ketchup! Or a tiny crumb! Or an even tinier crumb!"

"SpongeBob, please!" barked Squidward. "Nobody wants to watch you do anything."

Just then a sports agent walked up to SpongeBob. "You know, son, millions of hockey fans would love to watch you do that!"

"Really?" asked SpongeBob, his eyes opening wide. "I'm afraid they couldn't all fit in the Krusty Krab. That would be against safety regulations."

The agent chuckled. "Oh, no, not here, son," he replied. "In the Bikini Bottom Rink-a-Dome! How would you like to play professional hockey?"

SpongeBob gasped. "Me? A pro hockey player?"

"Sure, kid!" answered the agent. "You're a natural! I've watched a lot of players handle a stick over the years, but you're the best I've ever seen! Just sign this contract."

"I can't believe it!" SpongeBob cried.

"Neither can I," Squidward groaned.

SpongeBob had just finished signing the contract when Mr. Krabs came out of his office. "SpongeBob, what are you doing?" he yelled. "You're supposed to be earning me more money!"

SpongeBob beamed. "Just signing up to play professional hockey, Mr. Krabs."

Mr. Krabs turned even redder than usual. "What?" he bellowed. "You've already got a job . . . as my fry cook!"

The agent stepped forward. "And who might you be?" he asked.

"I be the owner and manager of this fine establishment," Mr. Krabs said proudly.

"Manager, eh?" the agent said. "Well, naturally, you're entitled to your cut." He slapped a big wad of cash into Mr. Krabs's claw.

For a moment Mr. Krabs just stood there, staring at the money. Then he started pushing SpongeBob out the door. "Don't just stand there! Go play hockey!"

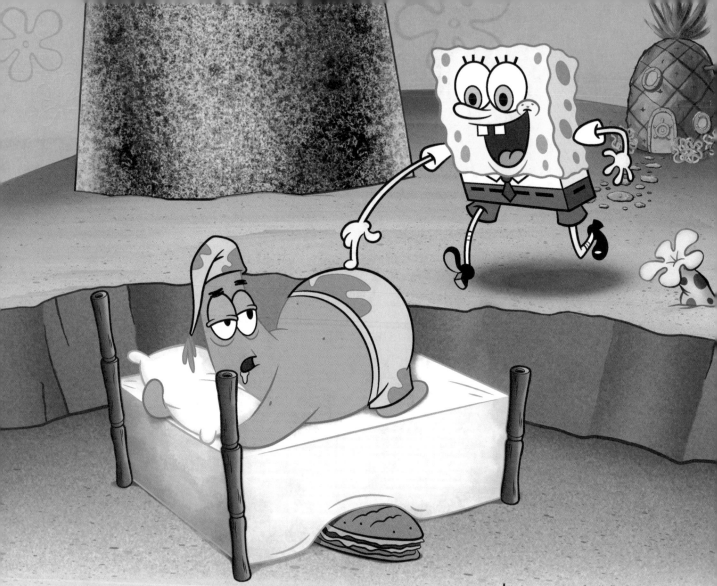

SpongeBob ran over to Patrick's house. "Hey, Patrick!" he called. "Guess what! I'm going to be a professional hockey player!"

Patrick was so excited, he got out of bed. "That's great, SpongeBob!"

"Yeah!" SpongeBob agreed. Then he admitted, "Only thing is, I've never played hockey in my life."

"No problem," Patrick said confidently. "I'll teach you everything you need to know!"

"Thanks, Patrick! I didn't know you played hockey," said SpongeBob.

Patrick grinned. "There are lots of things you don't know about me, SpongeBob."

"Like what?" SpongeBob asked.

Patrick thought hard. "Like I . . . um . . . uh . . . I can . . . play hockey!"

Patrick taught SpongeBob how to handle the hockey stick, pass, and shoot. They practiced for hours. Soon SpongeBob could put the puck in the goal from just about anywhere in Squidward's front yard.

"You're doing great, SpongeBob!" Patrick cheered.

"Only because I have such a good teacher," SpongeBob answered with a grin. "So when do we get to practice on ice?"

"What for?" Patrick asked, puzzled.

Before SpongeBob could answer, Squidward burst out his front door. "SpongeBob! Patrick! Stop playing hockey in my yard!" he yelled.

"What's Squidward so upset about?" Patrick asked.

"I think he wants me to get used to all the screaming fans," SpongeBob replied. He turned and waved. "Thanks, Squidward!"

The next day SpongeBob went down to the Bikini Bottom Rink-a-Dome to meet the coach.

"So you're the new kid, huh?" the coach said, looking SpongeBob up and down. "I hear you're good with a stick. Are you ready to play?"

SpongeBob took a deep breath. "I'm ready!" he said.

The coach slapped him on the back. "That's what I like to hear! Come on, let's get you suited up!"

Admiring his new uniform, SpongeBob pointed to his jersey and asked, "What does 'CB' stand for? Chilly Boys?"

The coach shook his head, chuckling. "No, that stands for our sponsor, the Chum Bucket."

SpongeBob's eyes widened. "The Chum Bucket? You mean, I'm playing hockey for Plankton?"

Just then Plankton stepped out of his office. "Is there a problem?" he gloated.

SpongeBob sputtered, "Yes, there's a problem! I can't play on your team! I work for the Krusty Krab! You're the enemy! You're evil!"

Plankton just laughed. "Oh, you'll play all right, SquarePants. You *have* to!" And he whipped out SpongeBob's signed contract.

SpongeBob gasped. Plankton was right. If he refused to play hockey for Plankton's team, SpongeBob would break his promise. And he couldn't do that.

SpongeBob had no choice. And he figured this wasn't about making Krabby Patties anyway; it was about playing hockey.

So he drew himself up and stood tall. "Okay, Plankton," SpongeBob said. "I am going to keep my promise. I'm going to play the best hockey I've ever played. . . . But you're still evil."

"Oh, SpongeBob, flattery will get you nowhere," Plankton replied with a smirk. "Now go!"

SpongeBob skated onto the ice for the pregame warm-ups. At first it felt strange—different from swatting garbage at the Krusty Krab and practicing in Squidward's front yard—but he soon got used to it.

He looked up at the stands and waved to Patrick. Then he looked over at the other team and saw . . . Sandy!

This is terrible, he thought. How can I play against one of my best friends?

SpongeBob tried to hide from Sandy, but she spotted him. "Howdy, SpongeBob!" she called, delighted. "What are you doing here?"

"Um, hi, Sandy," SpongeBob said nervously. "I'm . . . well, I'm . . . playing for the other team. I'm sorry!"

Sandy smiled. "Aw, you have nothing to be sorry about, SpongeBob!"
SpongeBob looked puzzled. "I don't?"
"Gosh, no!" Sandy exclaimed. "There's nothing better than a little
friendly competition. Why, it's no different than when we practice our
karate!"

SpongeBob felt better. "I guess you're right," he said.

Sandy patted him on the back. "The game's about to start. When that puck hits the ice, I want you to play all out. Go out there and have fun! Ya got that?"

"Yes, I do!" SpongeBob cried. "This is going to be the greatest hockey game ever, Sandy!"

And it was a great game! Both teams zipped up and down the ice scoring goals. SpongeBob scored twice, and so did Sandy.

In fact, it seemed as though every time the Chum Bucket team scored, the other team came right back at them and scored too!

Plankton cheered loudly from the sidelines. "Go, Chum Bucket team! Win! Conquer! Destroy!"

SpongeBob looked up at the scoreboard. The game was tied, and there were only seconds left. Could he score again before time ran out?

The other team had the puck, but suddenly one of SpongeBob's Chum Bucket teammates took it and started racing toward the goal. SpongeBob skated along with him, going as fast as he could.

"Here, SpongeBob!" the teammate called as he passed the puck to SpongeBob. Not wasting a second, SpongeBob headed for the goal.

Suddenly Sandy was by his side, trying to take the puck away, but SpongeBob slid it behind him, spun around, faked twice, and slapped it . . . into the net!

Goal! The buzzer sounded. The game was over, and the Chum Bucket team had won—thanks to SpongeBob!

"I win! I win!" Plankton shrieked.

As SpongeBob's teammates carried him on their shoulders, he looked over and saw Plankton celebrating.

SpongeBob smiled. "I guess even Plankton deserves to be happy now and then," he said.